P9-AQD-648

Chaela

This Ladybird Book belongs to:

Deanna

chantler,

I hate

this book

Chaela

This Ladybird retelling
by
Nicola Baxter

Ladybird books are widely available, but in case of
difficulty may be ordered by post or telephone from:

Ladybird Books – Cash Sales Department
Littlegate Road Paignton Devon TQ3 3BE
Telephone 0803 554761

A catalogue record for this book is available
from the British Library

First edition

Published by Ladybird Books Ltd Loughborough Leicestershire UK
Ladybird Books Inc Auburn Maine 04210 USA

Printed in England

FAVOURITE TALES

Cinderella

illustrated
by
JON DAVIS

based on the story by Charles Perrault

Once upon a time there was a young girl called Cinderella.

She lived with her father and two stepsisters. While her stepsisters spent their time buying pretty new clothes and going to parties, Cinderella wore old, ragged clothes and had to do all the hard work in the house.

The two sisters were selfish, unkind girls, which showed in their faces. Even wearing their fine clothes, they never looked as sweet and pretty as Cinderella.

One day a royal messenger came to announce that there was to be a grand ball at the King's palace.

The ball was in honour of the Prince, the King's only son.

Cinderella's sisters were both excited. The Prince was very handsome, and he had not yet found a bride.

When the evening of the ball arrived, Cinderella had to help her sisters get ready.

"Fetch my gloves!" cried one sister.

"Where are my jewels?" shrieked the other.

They didn't think for a minute that Cinderella might like to go to the ball!

When her sisters had driven off in their fine carriage, Cinderella sat all by herself and cried bitterly.

"Why are you crying, my dear?" said a voice. Cinderella looked up and was amazed to see her fairy godmother smiling down at her.

"I wish *I* could go to the ball and meet the Prince," Cinderella said, wiping away her tears.

"Then you shall!" laughed her fairy godmother. "But you must do exactly as I say."

"Oh, I *will*," promised Cinderella.

"Then go into the garden and fetch the biggest pumpkin you can find," said the fairy.

So Cinderella found an enormous pumpkin and brought it to her fairy godmother. With a wave of her magic wand, the fairy changed the pumpkin into a wonderful golden coach.

"Now bring me six white mice from the kitchen," the godmother said. Cinderella did as she was told.

Waving her wand again, the fairy godmother changed the mice into six gleaming white horses to pull the coach! Cinderella rubbed her eyes in amazement.

Then Cinderella looked down at her old ragged clothes. "Oh dear!" she sighed. "How can I go to the ball in this old dress?"

For the third time, her godmother waved her magic wand. In a trice, Cinderella was wearing a lovely white ballgown trimmed with blue silk ribbons. There were jewels in her hair, and on her feet were dainty glass dancing slippers.

"Now off you go!" said her fairy godmother, smiling. "Just remember one thing – the magic only lasts until midnight!"

So Cinderella went off to the ball in her sparkling golden coach.

In the royal palace, everyone was enchanted by the beautiful girl in the white and blue dress. "Who *is* she?" they whispered.

The Prince thought Cinderella was
the loveliest girl he had ever seen.

"May I have the honour of this
dance?" he asked, bowing low.

All the other girls were jealous of the
mysterious stranger.

Cinderella danced with the Prince all evening. She forgot her fairy godmother's warning until... *dong... dong... dong...* the clock began to strike midnight... *dong... dong... dong...*

Cinderella ran from the ballroom without a word... *dong... dong... dong...*

In her hurry, she lost one of her glass slippers... *dong... dong... dong.* The Prince ran out just as the lovely girl slipped out of sight.

"I don't even know her name," he sighed.

When Cinderella's sisters arrived home from the ball, they could talk of nothing but the beautiful girl who had danced with the Prince all evening.

"You can't imagine how annoying it was!" they cried. "After the wretched girl left in such a hurry, he wouldn't dance at all!"

Cinderella hardly heard their complaining. Her head and her heart were whirling with memories of the handsome Prince who had held her in his arms.

Meanwhile, the Prince was determined to find the mysterious beauty who had stolen his heart. The glass slipper was the only clue he had.

"The girl whose foot will fit this slipper shall be my wife," he said.

So the Prince set out to search the kingdom for his bride. A royal messenger carried the slipper on a silk cushion.

Every girl in the land wanted to try on the slipper. But although many tried, the slipper was always too small and too dainty.

At last the Prince came to Cinderella's house.

Each ugly sister in turn tried to squeeze her foot into the elegant slipper, but it was no use. Their feet were far too big and clumsy.

"Do you have any other daughters?" the Prince asked Cinderella's father.

"One more," he replied.

"Oh no," cried the sisters. "She is much too busy in the kitchen!" But the Prince insisted that *all* the sisters must try the slipper.

Cinderella hung her head in shame.
She did not want the Prince to see her
in her old clothes. But she sat down
and tried on the dainty slipper. Of
course, it fitted her perfectly!

The Prince looked at Cinderella's
sweet face and recognised the girl
he had danced with. "It *is* you," he
whispered. "Please be my bride, and
we shall never be parted again."

How happy Cinderella was! Her fairy
godmother appeared and, waving her
magic wand, dressed Cinderella
in a gown fit for a princess.

Then the Prince led
Cinderella home
to the royal palace.

Cinderella and her Prince were married at the most magnificent wedding that anyone could remember. Kings and queens from many lands came to meet the new Princess and wish her well.

Even Cinderella's sisters had to agree that she was the loveliest bride they had ever seen.

And Cinderella and her Prince lived
happily ever after.